window – I've seen her spring from the top of a sack of flour and catch the sparrow in flight."

"Oh, father, how horrid!" cried the miller's little daughter.

"Cats will be cats, my dear," said the miller.

The miller's family did not particularly like cats – they kept dogs in their own house – but they respected Old Belle. She was a business cat. Her public business was the keeping down of rats and mice in the mill. She ate what she caught, so that she had a double satisfaction. She was not one of those cats who go slipping away through the orchard grasses to see friends up in the village. Old Belle's friends had to come to the mill, if they wanted her. Only in summer she made short expeditions to the mill-house garden, to lie in the clumps of catmint in flower, until someone from the mill-house shouted to her to be gone. She knew the outside of the mill-house, but she had never wanted to go inside. Even when the house doors stood open in the sun, she gave only a glance inside on her way to the catmint border. She only wanted to be sure there was no dog there, waiting to rush out.

Old Belle's private business was to have kittens. In spite of her age, she had them regularly still, but nowadays in a rather desperate, devil-may-care manner. She chose to have them in the oddest places. A basket of eggs in the miller's office had been the most unfortunate choice from everyone's point of view. Whatever place she chose, the kittens were always found, and the miller always saw to it that all but one were drowned immediately.

"We can't have a plague of cats," he used to say.

He never let Old Belle guess what had become of her kittens, and the miller's little daughter never knew either. She thought that Old Belle had just one kitten at a time. The little girl used to play with that solitary kitten, until it was half grown. Then she gave it away to some good home in the village.

All the men in the mill where Old Belle worked had a fortnight's holiday every summer. Some took their holiday at one time, some at

another. In that way, the mill never needed to shut down. Old Belle, of course, was always on duty. Summer holidays were something she never took, and never noticed others taking – until one summer. That year, the milling business was unusually slack, and the miller decided to try an experiment: everybody should have his holiday at the same time, and the mill would shut down altogether for a fortnight. The miller and his whole family, with the dogs, would shut up house and go to the seaside.

Before he went, the miller hired an old man to go down to the mill every day to see that all was well – to see that boys were not breaking the mill-windows or interfering with the river-gates above the mill. Old Soldier Scar had the job.

"Oh, and there's another thing," the miller said to him. "There's the mill-cat."

"That one-eyed, scrawny beauty?" said Old Soldier Scar.

"See that she has a saucer of milk now and then. We always give her that. And she's going to have kittens, I think. Find out where she has them, and get rid of all but the prettiest one. Get

rid of them while they're very small. I want them gone when I get back."

"Dead and gone?" said Old Soldier Scar.

"Dead and buried," said the miller.

The next day he and his family all went off to the seaside. The mill stood silent and shut; the mill-house was the same.

At first Old Belle thought this quietness was a weekend, but it went on longer than a weekend – much longer. The only person she saw was Old Soldier Scar, and she did not see him every day. He rarely left her milk, after all, because he was secretly afraid of going inside the old mill. It was so empty, and dark, and silent except for the faintest rustle that might be the river underneath, and sudden creakings that nobody could explain, unless they were the comings and goings of the ghosts of hundreds of years of millers and cats and mice and rats.

Old Belle did not mind the lack of milk: there was always plenty for her to catch and eat. She did not mind the solitude at first. But after a while she began to have the oddest sensations. She would stop in the midst of her prowlings to listen for any sound that was not the squeaking of rats and mice or the creaking of old wood.

Never a sound of human voice or footfall: always silence. She was already feeling in a very unsettled state anyway, since she was about to have kittens, and now the strangeness of no one's ever being about began to get on her nerves.

She roamed the mill from top to bottom to find the perfect place to have her kittens, and in the end rushed out into the mill-garden and had them in an old seed-box by the tool-shed.

There were seven kittens, as healthy and handsome as her kittens always were, but they only worried her. She began carrying them back into the mill, and then changed her mind and brought them back to the seed-box again.

She had a look round the outside of the mill-house, but it was all shut up; not a sound. She went back to the seed-box and found that the kittens, in crawling round, had broken through the rotten wooden bottom of the box. She knew this was the wrong place for her kittens. She must not leave them here.

She went off to the mill-house again, and sniffed her way round at every door and at every low window-sill: all tightly shut. Then she came to the out-houses. Brushing along the wall of a lean-to shed, she found a loose boarding. She pushed her head behind it, and then her body, and wormed her way right through.

At first she seemed no better off, for she found herself in a dusty cinder-shed built against the brick wall of the mill-house. There was a great bulge in that wall, however, where a chimney was on the other side. Behind part of the bulge was a winding hole in the brickwork – something to do with the ventilation, perhaps.

Old Belle crept through the hole and came out beside a disused copper in a wash-house. From here she nosed a door open and stepped along a flagged passage into a kitchen. She was really inside the mill-house now. She was inside a house for the first time in her life.

The smell struck her most forcibly. She had smelt human beings before, but never so overwhelmingly. The chairs, the table – everything smelt of their touch, even of days ago. It was so different from the smell of the mill – the warm, nourishing smell of flour in the air, and the little thrilling currents of rat-smell. Here there was none of that.

She stepped over to the open door into the hall, and was met by such a violent smell of dog that she stiffened for battle. But there was no dog in the flesh, only the heavy waves of smell coming from an empty sleeping-box in a corner.

Down the hall she stepped delicately, going from door to door. Only one was open: Old Belle walked into the drawing-room. The blinds were down to save the photographs on the wall from the strong sunlight: the room was dim and had a heavy, drowsy air. A bluebottle buzzed

between the blind and the window. The eight-day grandfather clock was still ticking.

Old Belle glided between the armchairs. She stopped beside one, crouched, and then stretched her forepaws up the upholstery and raked her claws down the whole length of it, again and again. She had never had such a treat before.

Then Old Belle slid round the corner of the chair towards the fireplace, where she smelt a familiar salty, tarry scent – the coal in the coal-scuttle. She loved coal, and only a few months

ago had had five kittens on the coal-heap of the mill engine-room. Now she leaped lightly into the coal-scuttle and tramped among the lumps and coal-dust.

After a while she left the coal-scuttle in a long leap on to the couch. The cushions of the couch were the softest things she had come across so far. She kneaded them thoughtfully with her paws, and began to wonder if this were the place to bring her kittens. Then there was a little sound from the fireplace: a flake of soot had fallen down the chimney on to the sticks and paper in the hearth. Old Belle prowled across again and got up upon the kindling and wondered if this were the place for her kittens, with the blue eye of the sky far up the chimney above them.

Then she found the right place: the work-basket. Old Belle settled down into it. She could feel the shapes of the cotton-reels and balls of wool beneath her, but that was not unpleasant.

While she was in the work-basket, the grandfather clock began to strike. In one leap Old Belle was on the back of an armchair, facing the clock, ready for whatever it might do next. All it did was to finish striking, and go back to its ticking. The strings of the piano vibrated gently after the strokes, and then, in time, went silent again. There was only the ticking and the buzzing of the bluebottle.

Gradually Old Belle's arched back came down and her fur smoothed again. She climbed down from the chair and examined the base of the clock-case. She reached the decision that it was a piece of machinery like the pieces of machinery in the mill. One had to be careful, but no more.

The luxury of the drawing-room seemed safe, and Old Belle went off to fetch her kittens. She brought them one by one, dangling from her jaws, through the hole in the cinder-shed, in behind the brickwork by the wash-house copper, through the kitchen and the hall, and so into the drawing-room. Before dusk, all seven kittens were in the work-basket. The place was soft and weatherproof and draughtproof. All that troubled Old Belle was the eerie quietness of the house. Not a squeak of rat or mouse. After a few days, not any kind of noise, for the grandfather clock stopped ticking for lack of being wound up, and the bluebottle died. Perfect silence.

There was one mouse in the house, but Old Belle ate that on the second day. She found it in the store-room and, in catching it, knocked over a number of tins and bottles. She tracked down some cheese that had been left breathing through a little hole in the top of its cheese-dish. She patted and pushed the cheese-dish with her paws until it fell off the shelf and she could pick out the cheese from among the fragments of broken china. There was more of the best quality food about, if Old Belle had only known – sardines and salmon in tins; but it was of no use to her. She had to go back to the mill for her usual hunting.

Old Soldier Scar glimpsed her once and tried to make her show where her kittens were hidden. When she ran from him out into the mill-garden, he did not believe her and stumped home swearing.

A week passed before Old Belle went upstairs in the mill-house. Perhaps – like many people who do daring things – she did it in the end because she was afraid.

What lay up there?

She climbed the stairs so softly that even the treacherous step third-from-the-bottom never creaked.

Along the landing, the bathroom door was shut, the lavatory door was shut, all the bedroom doors were shut, except one.

She walked in.

This was the room where the miller and his wife slept, in a big double bed that faced a big wardrobe. In one of the doors of the wardrobe was a full-length mirror.

Old Belle crossed the carpet, paused a moment to feel the fleeciness of the bedside rug, and then jumped on to the bed. Light-footed as she was, she sank into the softness of the eiderdown. The place was softer and warmer than anything downstairs.

She walked about on the eiderdown, trying it for her kittens. She had reached the foot of the bed when she became aware of something in the room besides herself, moving. There was neither sound nor smell of living creature, and yet she saw movement. Yes, there it was; and she knew the kind of movement, too – a cat's. Advancing towards her was the most alarming cat that Old Belle had ever seen – big, bony, strong-looking, a little mad-looking, and with one eyelid drooping in a dreadful, ceaseless wink. Old Belle arched her back. The other cat arched its back, too, with the greatest enmity. Old Belle stared and stared, but the other cat never faltered under her gaze.

There is a time when retreat is not cowardice. Old Belle slowly drew back first one paw, then another. She began to move backwards over the eiderdown. She was afraid that the other cat might follow up its advantage; but it withdrew into the shadows whence it had come. Meanwhile Old Belle let herself quietly down to the floor by the coverlet, and very quickly walked over to the doorway and through.

She ran quickly and quietly downstairs to her kittens again. She lay relaxed among them, but she hushed them when they mewed. She was listening for any sound from upstairs. Nothing.

In the following days, Old Belle perhaps forgot what she had seen upstairs. She could not forget, however, the feel of the eiderdown on the bed. Who could forget such softness! The work-basket was comfortable for her kittens, but the eiderdown – ah! she dreamed of it!

At last Old Belle picked up the first kitten for a move upstairs. The bedroom door was still open. The bedroom was quiet and scentless, except for the fading smell of the human beings who usually slept there.

Old Belle, her kitten in her mouth, gathered herself together on the bedside rug and then, leaping, gained the height of the bed, and felt the eiderdown beneath her. It was no less soft than she had remembered. She rejoiced. Before she put her kitten down, she looked around her.

And then – there was the other cat again! Moreover, as if it had known what Old Belle intended, and as if it wanted to stake out its own right, the other cat was bringing its own kitten

to exactly the same spot.

Old Belle was always more warlike when she had any of her kittens with her. Now she might have set the kitten down and advanced to fight, but for a strange kind of fear that was creeping over her. She noticed once more that the cat had no smell or sound. Old Belle's kitten – well-grown and lusty by now – wriggled as it hung from her jaws, and squeaked. The kitten of the other cat wriggled too, and its mouth opened

and closed; but it gave no sound. Soundless, scentless, unearthly, the witch-cat with its witch-kitten glared at Old Belle.

Old Belle's nerve broke all at once. With one great spring, her kitten still in her jaws, she went from the bed to the door; through it, down the stairs, and – without going back to her other kittens – through the kitchen, the wash-house, the cinder-shed, back to the old seed-box, where she dropped her kitten.

One kitten saved.

One by one, the other kittens were fetched into safety. Old Belle never stopped for rest or consideration. Only, each time she passed through the hall of the mill-house, she paused a second to listen for any sound from upstairs. She

hardly knew what she expected – perhaps the echoing pad of a monstrous, one-eyed witch-cat coming down. Always, upstairs, there was total silence.

The seed-box was only a half-way place for the kittens; it was still too near the mill-house for Old Belle's peace of mind. All the kittens had to be carried on into the mill. After that, Old Belle did not much care where she put them. The miller's market-bag was open, and there, on top of corn-samples and entry-books, she gathered her family into a real home at last. The place was unfamiliar to the kittens, and by no means as comfortable as the work-basket had been. They whimpered a little before they fell asleep.

Old Belle paid no attention to them. She watched the moon rise. She watched the shadows of night creeping out from the dark corners of the old mill. She snuffed the smell of corn and cobwebs, with the faint, dank smell of the mill-stream below. She listened to the cry and scamper of rats and mice, and the mysterious creaking of old timbers in an old mill. She felt safe at home.

The next day the miller's family came back from holiday. In the mill, the miller found Old Belle with a family of kittens so well-grown that, really, one could not think of drowning any of them. He only wondered where she had managed to hide them from Old Soldier Scar.

In the mill-house, the miller's wife found her drawing-room in the strangest mess, with coal-marks and soot-marks everywhere, the upholstery of one of her best chairs in tatters, and the cottons and wools of her work-basket in such confusion that they had to be thrown away in one tangled lump. Someone or something had been in her store-room, too.

Upstairs, in the big bed-room, the miller and his wife never noticed the very slight crumpling

of the eiderdown, where Old Belle had walked and stood. When they turned to the mirror in the wardrobe, they saw only their own faces and figures. The mirror told them nothing of what it had reflected in their absence.

The miller and his wife never thought of connecting the odd occurrences in the mill and in the mill-house. As for the miller's little girl, she remembers still that remarkable summer when, for the first time, Old Belle had seven pretty kittens, instead of only one.

First published in 1989 by
André Deutsch Limited
105-106 Great Russell Street, London WC1B 3LJ

Second impression 1990

British Library Cataloguing in Publication Data

Pearce, Philippa
Old Belle's summer holiday.
I. Title II. Geldart, William, *1936-*
823′.914 [J]

ISBN 0 233 98176 4